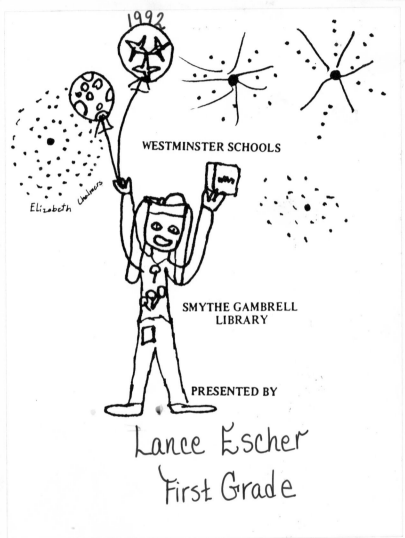

1992

WESTMINSTER SCHOOLS

Elizabeth Chalmers

SMYTHE GAMBRELL
LIBRARY

PRESENTED BY

Lance Escher
First Grade

The Black Cat

ALLAN AHLBERG · ANDRÉ AMSTUTZ

GREENWILLOW BOOKS, NEW YORK

Printed in Great Britain by
Cambus Litho, East Kilbride

Library of Congress Cataloging-in-Publication Data
Ahlberg, Allan.   The black cat.
Summary: A little black cat watches the antics
of three skeletons sledding in the snow.
[1. Skeleton—Fiction.   2. Snow—Fiction.
3. Cats—Fiction]   I. Amstutz, André, ill.
II. Title.   PZ7.A2688B1   1990   [E]
90-2886   ISBN 0-688-09903-3.
ISBN 0-688-09904-1 (lib. bdg.)

In a dark dark town,
on a cold cold night,
under a starry starry sky,
down a slippery slippery slope,
on a bumpety bumpety sled . . .

a little skeleton is sliding . . .
and sliding . . .
and crashing – wallop!

The little skeleton
loses a leg in the snow.
A white leg in snow
is hard to find.
A black cat in snow
is easy to find.
What is she doing here?

The little skeleton and the big skeleton
go to the boneyard
to get a new leg
for the little skeleton.

They play around with the bones
for a while . . .
and go home to bed.

Then . . .
in the dark dark town,
on <u>another</u> cold cold night,
under a starry starry sky,
down a slippery slippery slope,
on a bumpety bumpety sled . . .

<u>two</u> skeletons are sliding . . .
and sliding . . .
and sliding . . .
and crashing — bang!
WALLOP!
This time the big skeleton
loses a leg in the snow.

A white leg in snow
is hard to find.
A black cat is easy.
Is she still here?
I wonder why.

The big skeleton
and the little skeleton
go to the boneyard
to get a new leg
for the big skeleton.

They play around again with the bones
and go home to bed.

Then . . .
in the dark town,
on the <u>next</u> night,
under a starry sky,
with a moon, too,
down a slippery slope,
in the frosty air,
on a bumpety sled . . .

three skeletons are sliding . . .
and sliding . . .
and shouting . . .
and barking!
And banging! Wallop! CRASH!

RASH!

This time the big skeleton
and the little skeleton
lose the dog skeleton.
A white dog in snow
is hard to find.
But a noisy dog is easy to find.
So is a black cat!

The dog skeleton chases the cat.
Now we know –
that's what she is here for!

The dog chases the cat
up and down
the dark dark hill,
in and out
of the dark dark boneyard,

BONE YARD

round and round
the dark dark streets
and down and down
to the dark dark cellar.